D0231859

URGENCY
EMERGENCY!
Injured Spider

Dosh Archer

BLOOMSBURY

LONDON BERLIN NEW YORK

It was another busy day at City
Hospital. Outside it was pouring
with rain. Doctor Glenda was
making an important phone call
and Nurse Percy was looking after
one of the King's men, whose foot
had been squashed by a huge egg.

Just then the ambulance arrived.

'Urgency Emergency!' called the Pengamedics. 'We have an injured spider here. Injured spider coming through!'

Miss Muffet was running beside the trolley. She was the one who had called the ambulance.

'I don't know what happened,' cried Miss Muffet. 'I was just walking along when I found the spider lying in a puddle of water at the bottom of the waterspout.

I'm afraid of spiders, but I couldn't just leave her lying there.'

'Step back!' cried Doctor Glenda.
'Let me examine her.

It is just as I thought. She is very badly injured. There's a cut on her head. Nurse Percy, put a pad over that cut to stop any more bleeding.'

'Can you tell me your name?' asked Doctor Glenda as she shone a special light into the spider's eyes.

'Incy Wincy,' said the spider.

'Good,' said Doctor Glenda. 'How many fingers am I holding up?'

'Two,' said Incy Wincy.
'That's right,' said Doctor
Glenda. 'You are in hospital
because you had some kind
of accident. Can you tell us
what happened?'

'I was just climbing up the waterspout,' said Incy. 'Then it started to rain . . .'

'The last thing I remember is a big whoosh of water rushing towards me.'

Doctor Glenda turned to Nurse Percy. 'It looks like she was knocked down the waterspout by a torrent of rain. I think her brain is OK, but now we must act quickly – that cut will need stitches.'

Incy trembled with fear. Nurse
Percy put an arm round her.
'Don't worry. It won't hurt a bit.'

Nurse Percy gave Incy a special
injection to stop the stitches hurting.

'I will do the stitches myself,' said
Doctor Glenda.
Nurse Percy brought the special
needle and thread.

Very carefully Doctor
Glenda made four tiny
stitches to hold the cut
together so that it could
get better.

Nurse Percy
held all of
Incy's hands.

Nurse Percy was right
– it didn't hurt a bit.

Then he put a special sticky plaster on the cut to keep it nice and clean so it could heal.

But now Incy was feeling a bit
wobbly.

'Is there anyone who can help you get home?' asked Nurse Percy.

Incy shook her head. 'My sister is on holiday,' she said.

Nurse Percy had an idea.

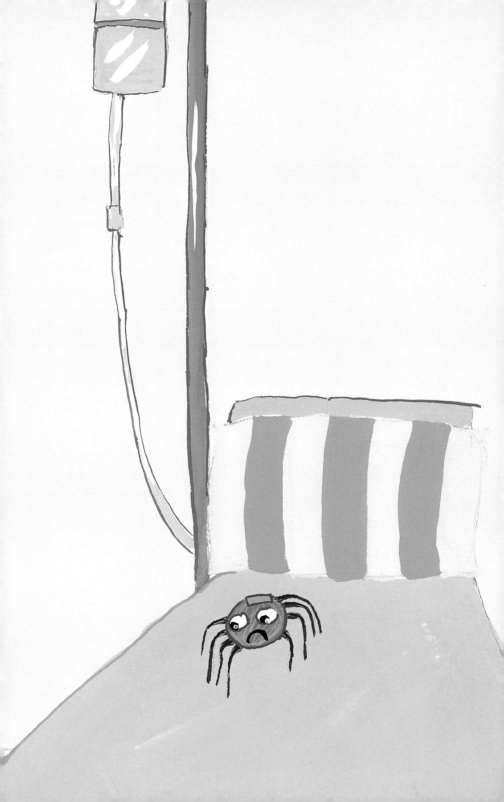

He went to speak to Miss Muffet.
'I know you are afraid of spiders,'
said Nurse Percy, 'but do you think
you could overcome your fears and
look after Incy just for tonight? She
will be feeling much
better tomorrow.'

Miss Muffet looked at poor Incy.

'Oh, all right then,' she said. 'Come on, Incy. I haven't got any flies for you to eat, but if you don't mind, you can have some of my curds and whey.'

'I can never thank you enough,' said Incy Wincy.

'All in a day's work,' said Doctor Glenda.

Outside the sun had come out
and dried up all the rain. Thanks
to Doctor Glenda and her team,
and with a little help from her new
friend, Miss Muffet, Incy Wincy the
spider would soon be climbing up
that waterspout again.

Enjoy more madcap first readers in the
URGENCY EMERGENCY! series . . .